CO-ALE-807

It was a time of LEGENDS. Kings and queens ruled the land.

It was a time of MAGIC. Fairies and other mythical beings cast spells—both good and evil.

And it was a time of HEROES. Four brave knights were sent on a quest to find a great warrior who the legends foretold would end a terrible war and bring peace for a hundred lifetimes.

It was the time of the MYSTIC KNIGHTS OF TIR NA NOG!

Go on all the
Mystic Knights adventures:

#1 THE LEGEND OF
THE ANCIENT SCROLL

#2 FIRE WITHIN, AIR ABOVE!

#3 WATER AROUND, EARTH BELOW!

#4 THE TAMING OF PYRE

#5 DRAGANTA REVEALED!*

*coming soon

ATTENTION: ORGANIZATIONS AND CORPORATIONS
HarperCollins books may be purchased for educational, business, or sales promotional use. For information please write: Special Markets Department, HarperCollins Publishers Inc., 10 East 53rd Street, New York, NY 10022-5299.

Book #4

The Taming
of Pyre

Written by John Whitman

■ HarperEntertainment
A Division of HarperCollinsPublishers

▲ HarperEntertainment

A Division of HarperCollins*Publishers*

10 East 53rd Street, New York, NY 10022-5299

If you purchased this book without a cover, you should be aware that this book is stolen property. It was reported as "unsold and destroyed" to the publisher and neither the author nor the publisher has received any payment for this "stripped book."

This is a work of fiction. The characters, incidents, and dialogues are products of the author's imagination, or if real, are used fictitiously. Any resemblance to actual events or persons, living or dead, is entirely coincidental.

™ © 1999 Saban Entertainment, Inc. and Saban International N.V. MYSTIC KNIGHTS OF TIR NA NOG and all related logos, names and distinctive likenesses are the exclusive property of Saban Entertainment, Inc. and Saban International N.V. All Rights Reserved.

No part of this book may be used or reproduced in any manner whatsoever without written permission except in the case of brief quotations embodied in critical articles and reviews. For information address HarperCollins Publishers Inc., 10 East 53rd Street, New York, NY 10022-5299.

First printing: September 1999

Cover illustration by Mel Grant
Designed by Susan Sanguily

Printed in the United States of America

ISBN 0–06–107163–3

HarperCollins®, ▲ ®, and HarperEntertainment™ are trademarks of HarperCollins Publishers Inc.

Visit HarperEntertainment on the World Wide Web at
http://www.harpercollins.com

10 9 8 7 6 5 4 3 2 1

Welcome, Great Seer

You, dear reader, are a powerful, mystical being known as the Great Seer of Tir na Nog. You can witness and control the fate of the four brave heroes in this story. This wondrous magical gift has always been within you. At several points in this tale you will be asked to make a choice . . . a choice that will affect the lives of not only Rohan, Ivar, Deirdre, and Angus, but also the entire kingdom. They need the guidance of your mystical powers.

But with great power comes great responsibility. So, Great Seer, use your gift wisely. For the destiny of the Mystic Knights of Tir na Nog—and the fate of the Kingdom of Kells—rests in your mighty hands!

History

Long ago, far across oceans, an island was divided into two kingdoms. The Kingdom of Kells was ruled by good King Conchobar. The Kingdom of Temra was ruled by the evil Queen Maeve. Queen Maeve believed that it was her birthright to rule the entire island. She would therefore not rest until her armies had conquered Kells.

King Conchobar's army fought fiercely, and the evil queen was stopped time and again. In desperation, Maeve turned to the dark magic of an evil fairy named Mider. Using the powers of sorcery given to her by Mider, Maeve conjured a host of terrible giants, ogres, and other mystical beasts to help her battle the armies of Kells. Aided by the creatures of darkness, Maeve's forces turned the tide of battle. It was a dark time for Kells, and King Conchobar even talked of surrender. All hope seemed lost . . .

But was it?

The king's trusted advisor, Cathbad the Druid, who possessed special powers, had raised an orphan named Rohan. Now eighteen and Cathbad's apprentice, Rohan had become a skilled swordsman. But Cathbad never told Rohan that there was an amazing secret about the young apprentice's destiny.

Cathbad had in his possession a piece of an

Ancient Scroll that spoke of the coming of a great warrior named Draganta, who would bring peace to the land. Now, in these desperate times, Cathbad revealed the scroll to Rohan . . . and showed him that a birthmark on Rohan's arm matched a symbol on the scroll!

Upon seeing this, and learning of the prophecy of the coming of Draganta, Rohan was convinced that he was the one to lead the quest to find the legendary warrior—the Kingdom of Kells's only hope.

Rohan is joined by Deirdre, King Conchobar's strong and beautiful daughter; Angus, Rohan's best friend; and Ivar, a prince from a faraway land across the sea. Together they must journey to Tir na Nog, the land beneath the Earth, where the magical wee folk live. With the help of Fin Varra, the wise but tricky King of Tir na Nog, the four young warriors must prove their worth so that they can become the MYSTIC KNIGHTS OF TIR NA NOG!

Now they must find the warrior Draganta and save the Kingdom of Kells!

Lexicon

ARTILLERY:
Weaponry, especially fired through the air.

BATTALION:
A group of soldiers, often on horseback.

CHALICE:
A fancy cup.

DOLMAN:
A magical formation of rocks.

DRUID:
A magician or seer.

IMPLORE:
To beg.

INVINCIBLE:
Cannot be defeated.

LEXICON:
A list of words.

MENTOR:
A teacher or counselor.

PROPHECY:
A prediction of the future.

SCEPTER:
A rod held by a ruler to signify royalty.

SUMMON:
To call into one's presence.

VETERAN:
An experienced warrior.

VULNERABLE:
Able to be hurt.

WAGER:
To bet.

THE TAMING OF PYRE

Dark mist settled over the Kingdom of Kells.

The mist was cold and damp, and it crept inside the armor of a band of Kells soldiers who guarded the border of the kingdom. The soldiers would have liked to go home to their warm fires and their families, but they didn't dare leave their posts.

Kells was at war with the Kingdom of Temra. Maeve, the Evil Queen who ruled Temra, had sworn to destroy Conchobar, the king of Kells. If the Kells warriors let down their guard for an instant, the enemy would attack.

One young soldier shuddered in the chilly air. "It's cold enough to send a shiver through the Otherworld and back," he said.

An older soldier beside him growled, "Aye, stop your bellyaching. Why, I've seen cold that would freeze your blood just to tell of it."

The young soldier kicked a stone. "Eerily quiet, it is."

The older man nodded. "True, but be thankful for that quiet. A good soldier always hopes for a quiet day. Why I remember back when wicked Queen Maeve first—"

A great war cry interrupted his words. The band of Kells warriors looked up to see a terrifying figure rise out of the mist.

"By all the magic in Kells!" the young soldier cried. "What's that?"

The old soldier took a step back. "Brace yourself, lad. That's Torc, Queen Maeve's Chief of Guards. And

I'll wager a wagon full of gold he's not alone!"

The veteran warrior was right. As Torc, dressed in dark armor, stalked forward, an entire battalion of Temran warriors appeared out of the mist behind him.

Torc threw back his head and roared, "Prepare for your defeat, you blasted Kellsmen!" He turned to his own warriors and raised a great battle sword. "Charge!" The Temran warriors let loose another war cry and surged forward. The Kells soldiers barely had time to draw their weapons before Torc and his men slammed into them. In seconds, swords and axes sliced through the thick mist as the sounds of battle filled the air.

The Kellsmen fought bravely, but they were outnumbered, and step by step the Temran warriors drove them back.

"We're done for!" cried the young Kells soldier.

"Not yet!" shouted the veteran. "Look!"

Out of the mist charged four more figures. But these were not more Temran warriors. They were the Mystic Knights—the heroes of Kells!

Rohan, the young apprentice who had become a great knight.

Angus, the thief-turned-hero, who fought beside his best friend Rohan.

Deirdre, the king's daughter, and one of the fiercest fighters in the land.

Ivar, the stranger from a distant land, who had joined the others after Rohan saved his life.

"Courage, men!" called the old soldier. "We've got a chance now!"

Rohan heard the old man's cry and smiled. "Did you hear that?"

Beside him, Angus nodded. "We wouldn't want to make a liar out of him, now would we?"

"Let's go!" Deirdre cried.

The Mystic Knights plunged into the battle. Staring down a horde of Temran warriors, Rohan drew a sword from his side. "Have a taste of the Sword of Kells!" he cried. Instantly, a blast of flame leaped from his sword, scattering Maeve's soldiers.

Beside him, Deirdre drew her own weapon. "My Whirlwind Crossbow will tame you Temrans." She fired, letting loose a magic whirlwind that hurled the Temran soldiers from their lines.

The first ranks of the invading army fell apart, and the Kellsmen cheered. But a fresh line of Temran warriors advanced, preparing to charge the Mystic Knights.

Angus stepped forward. "Don't forget about my Terra Mace—"

"Or my Barbed Trident!" Ivar added. Both heroes used their weapons at once. The Terra Mace exploded like an earthquake that hurled Temran soldiers from their feet, while the Barbed Trident sent a lightning bolt sizzling through the enemy ranks.

In moments the Temran attack had stalled. Torc's soldiers hesitated, staring in fear at the Mystic Knights and their magic weapons. Then with a single cry of terror they turned and fled.

Torc's face turned bright red with rage. "Where are you cowards going?" he shouted at his retreating army. "They're only four scrawny children! Get back here!"

He might as well have shouted at the mist, for the Temran soldiers kept running for their lives. Torc cursed them once again, then turned to face the Kellsmen. He was alone now against a band of soldiers and the Mystic Knights, but he still glared at them as though ready to fight.

Just as the heroes prepared to advance, Torc spat, "You haven't seen the last of me!" Then he too turned and vanished into the mist.

The soldiers of Kells let out a cheer of victory.

Turn to page 18

Rohan looked north toward the Caves of Dare. "I think our true quest lies with the dragon Pyre."

All the Mystic Knights agreed, and they quickly set out toward the dragon's lair. Before long they could see the caves again. Smoke billowed out of the cave mouth. Now and then a flash of dragon fire lit the inside of the cave like lightning.

"I hope we can tame that dragon this time," Angus muttered.

Rohan nodded. "I have a feeling everything is going to work out fine."

"Or maybe not," Angus said. "Look!"

The four Evil Sentinels seemed to melt out of the rocks. The Ice Lord, the Rock Wolf, the Sea Serpent, and the Lightning Bat surrounded the young heroes.

"Greetings, Mystic Knights," the Lightning Bat screeched.

"And farewell!" the Ice Lord added. "Prepare for your final battle!"

Rohan leaped forward to meet the Evil Sentinel's

6

charge. Ice met fire as the Sword of Kells clanged against the Black Ice Sword. "Your sword skills have not improved since our last encounter," the Ice Lord said with a grin. The Evil Sentinel faked a sword thrust, then kicked Rohan in the chest, sending the Mystic Knight sprawling across the ground.

Nearby, Angus battled the Rock Wolf, fending off blows from the Wolf's Tooth Claw.

"Ready to give up, little warrior?" Rock Wolf growled.

"Nope," Angus replied. "You forgot to say please." Swinging his Terra Mace, he managed to drive the Rock Wolf back. They circled one another again.

Ivar ducked beneath a blow of the Serpent Tongue Whip as Deirdre sent Lightning Bat sprawling with a powerful kick. "It would help if we had our armor!" she called.

Rohan climbed to his feet. "I'll give us a chance."

The Sword of Kells roared and flames leaped up in great sheets. A wall of fire rose between the Mystic Knights and the Evil Sentinels.

Turn to page 23

Rohan looked each of the others in the eye. "Let's stay and see if we can make the dragon wear himself out," he said. "But in case I'm wrong about this, there's no sense in all of us risking our lives."

Without another word, the young hero strode up to the enormous dragon. "All right, Pyre. Bring it on!"

The great dragon reared back its head, then jabbed it forward, spewing a great stream of fire. The blast threw Rohan off his feet . . . but his Mystic Armor protected him from harm. Groaning, Rohan climbed back onto his feet. "Is that the best you can do?" he challenged.

Pyre roared and gathered himself for an even greater blast. When he unleashed his fire, it was as though a volcano had erupted. Rohan vanished behind a wall of flame. The other Mystic Knights could only watch in horror.

Turn to page 34

On the far side of the field, the Mystic Knights let out a cheer. They had only been pretending not to notice the Evil Sentinels. Their argument was meant to make them look vulnerable to an attack.

Aideen appeared in the air and flew over to Rohan, who smiled at her. "Good job, Aideen. Your plan worked!"

Aideen beamed. "Of course. I was very convincing."

"Now, about our weapons?" Ivar said. "We can't go into that field to get them."

"Don't worry!" Aideen replied with a laugh. "I'll take care of that, too!"

The fairy turned and flew out over the field to get their weapons.

Before long the Mystic Knights had their weapons once more.

Rohan smiled at Aideen. "Sometimes good things come in small packages!"

"Oh, it's good to see you again!" Angus said, kissing his Terra Mace.

Ivar held up his Barbed Trident and grinned. "I think I'd rather use my trident on the Sea Serpent than kiss it."

"How can we ever repay you, Aideen?" Rohan asked.

The fairy blushed. "You'll think of something, Rohan. For now, good-bye. And good luck with the dragon!"

She zipped away as quick as a lost thought.

The Mystic Knights set out once again for the Caves of Dare.

Turn to page 20

The Mystic Knights watched nervously as the dragon roared and spouted great fountains of flame. Then, as quickly as he had appeared, Pyre retreated back into his cave.

Angus groaned. "He's gone back inside. How do we approach him now?"

"We go in after him," Rohan said, his voice full of determination.

"We go in after him?" Angus repeated in disbelief. Then he realized the others had already started toward the cave. He sighed. "Aye, we go in after him."

The Mystic Knights had faced Pyre once before, and they had failed to tame him then. The memory did not sit easily with any of them.

"He looks wilder than ever," Deirdre whispered as they reached the edge of the cave.

Rohan shrugged. "He can be as wild as he wants. This time we have our Mystic Armor." Raising his voice, Rohan called out his personal magic phrase. "Fire within me!"

In a brilliant flash of multicolored light, Rohan's simple coat of chain mail was transformed into a magnificent suit of Mystic Armor that almost nothing could penetrate.

"Air above me!" Deirdre cried.

"Earth beneath me!" Angus shouted.

"Water around me!" Ivar called.

Following their chants, each hero was bathed in shimmering light and then encased within their Mystic Armor.

Through the face mask of his shining helmet, Rohan said, "Let's split up."

The Mystic Knights strode into the cave. Pyre lay in the middle of the stone chamber, watching closely as the four heroes surrounded him on all sides. As the Knights charged forward, the great dragon moved with incredible speed, turning to blow smoke and fire at them before they could reach him. Each hero was knocked backward and fell heavily to the ground.

"That didn't work," Angus groaned.

"Let's all grab him by the tail and hang on!" Ivar shouted.

Once again they charged, this time diving for the dragon's tail. Pyre roared angrily and stomped his feet, whirling around and thrashing his tail as the Knights held on for dear life. But even they could not hang on for long. With a snap of his tail, the dragon hurled them off and the Mystic Knights fell in one great heap.

"That didn't work either," Angus groaned again.

Deirdre climbed to her feet. "I think this may require a woman's approach. Something soft and gentle."

She strode forward until she was face-to-face with the dragon. As Pyre eyed her suspiciously, Deirdre said gently, "There, there, now . . . there's nothing to be scared of. See, I'm your friend."

The princess petted his snout softly. As she did, Pyre opened his mouth and belched right in Deirdre's face!

Deirdre wrinkled her nose at the stench. "Why you impudent lizard!" she cried, and she punched the dragon in the snout.

"So much for the soft and gentle approach," Rohan said with a laugh.

Pyre roared in pain and let loose another blast of fire that scorched the air over the heroes' heads.

Angus drew his Terra Mace. "I think it's time to bring out the heavy artillery."

The others followed his example. The Mystic Knights leveled their weapons at the dragon. One after the other they let loose their magic. Fierce fire, powerful whirlwinds, bone-jarring explosions, and bolts of lightning all streaked toward Pyre. But the powerful energy either bounced off the dragon's scaly hide or slowed him for only a moment.

The mystic weapons only had one true effect.

They made the dragon even more angry!

Pyre reared back, then lunged his long neck forward, snapping at the heroes, who scrambled to get out of his reach.

Pressed back against the cave wall, Deirdre shouted, "It's no use! We can't tame this thing!"

Rohan nodded. "Aye, we'd better go to that fairy king Fin Varra in Tir na Nog . . . and fast! He's got some explaining to do!"

Angus frowned. "I don't trust Fin Varra. Besides, we're supposed to tame this dragon ourselves."

Ivar ducked as a sheet of fire roared overhead, scorching the rocks behind him. "We'd better decide before we're turned into roast!"

Turn the page

Great Seer of Tir na Nog,

the Mystic Knights need your help! You must decide what course of action they take.

If you think the heroes should try again to tame Pyre on their own, go to page 15.

If you think they should journey to Tir na Nog to seek help, go to page 58.

15

"**A**ll right, then," Rohan said, raising his sword. "If we're going to tame Pyre, let's do it now!"

The Mystic Knights charged forward, ready to unleash the power of their weapons. But Pyre was too quick for them. The dragon lashed out with his tail, smashing Ivar in the chest, hurling him through the air. The blow was so powerful that Ivar was thrown right out of the cave.

"Ivar!" Rohan cried. Forgetting Pyre, he turned and ran after his friend with the others close behind.

Rohan expected to find Ivar somewhere just outside the cave, but the Mystic Knight of Water and his Barbed Trident were nowhere to be seen.

"By all the gold in Kells!" Angus gasped. "That dragon's hurled Ivar right off the edge of the world!"

"No!" Ivar's voice called out. "Just off the edge of this cliff!"

The voice had come from down the mountainside. The other Mystic Knights quickly followed Ivar's calls until they came to the edge of a steep cliff. Leaning over carefully, they saw Ivar about ten feet down the side of the cliff, clinging to a ledge with one hand. Below him was a drop of two hundred feet.

"Are you all right?" Rohan called down.

"I've been better!" Ivar called up. "If it weren't for this Mystic Armor, that blow would have smashed me to a pulp!"

"How do we get him up?" Deirdre asked Rohan and Angus. "We don't have any rope."

"You'll be the rope," Rohan told her. "Lean over the side. Angus and I will hold your legs and Ivar can use you to climb up."

Deirdre looked shocked. "You must be joking."

"Could you hurry up there!" Ivar shouted.

"We're discussing strategy," Angus joked. "Hang on a second."

"Very funny!" Ivar yelled back.

Deirdre glanced over the side. "Okay, I'll do it. But if you fellows drop me, I'll come back to haunt you as a ghost who screams at you forever."

"How is that different than any normal day?" Angus asked.

"Hurry!" Ivar called.

Diedre leaned over the side, with the two other Knights holding her in place. She stretched down . . . and was still a few feet short of Ivar's hand. But Ivar raised his Barbed Trident, which Diedre grasped easily. "Pull!"

Angus and Rohan pulled, dragging Deirdre, the Trident, and Ivar up all at once.

"Whew!" Rohan said. "That was a big job."

"Um . . ." Angus said as a shadow fell across them. "Not as big as this one!"

The other Mystic Knights glanced up to see a gigantic Ogre standing over them. The Ogre snarled, revealing a few hooked and yellow teeth. Then he raised an enormous club, nearly the size of a tree, and brought it crashing down.

All four heroes rolled away just in time, and jumped to their feet with their weapons drawn. "His home must be around here somewhere," Rohan guessed. "We're probably intruding."

"How impolite of us," Angus said. "Let's not overstay our welcome!"

The Ogre roared again, but before he could strike, the Mystic Knights had scrambled up the hill toward the Caves of Dare. The Ogre chased after them, but as soon as the heroes approached Pyre's cave again, the giant monster gave up and retreated.

"That Ogre's smarter than we are," Angus said. "He's not foolish enough to get near Pyre's cave."

"We don't have any choice," Rohan said. He started to enter the cave again. "Well, shall we try one more time?"

From the shadows of his cave, Pyre heard Rohan's voice and let out a roar that shook the mountainside. Flames swirled out from the cave's depths.

Angus gulped. "You know, visiting Fin Varra isn't looking so bad after all."

Turn to page 58

Ever since Rohan and his friends had gained their magic weapons, and the Mystic Armor that gave them protection, they had been nearly invincible. The Mystic Knights had succeeded in turning back Maeve's powerful army several times. But as they rode toward the Kells castle, Rohan cautioned himself against becoming too confident. Maeve had dark forces of evil at her command, and sooner or later she would find a way to defeat Kells.

Rohan knew that the only way to make sure the kingdom was safe was to fulfill an ancient legend. This legend foretold of a great warrior named Draganta who would come to defend Kells and bring peace for a hundred lifetimes.

The Mystic Knights had already fulfilled part of the legendary quest to find Draganta—they had earned their weapons in the mysterious land of Tir na Nog, and had battled the four Evil Sentinels in order to win their Mystic Armor. But before Draganta could be revealed, the heroes had to complete one other part of the prophecy.

King Conchobar received the Mystic Knights in his throne room. Beside him stood Cathbad, the wise druid who had been Rohan's mentor.

The king smiled at the four young heroes. "Another hard-fought and victorious battle."

"Ah . . ." Angus yawned as though he'd done all the work. "It was nothing."

"My king," Rohan said, "now that we each have our Mystic Armor and weapons, the time has come for us to tame the dragon Pyre."

Cathbad the Druid nodded. "So the legend says. Draganta cannot be discovered until the Four Heroes have tamed the dragon."

"His lair is hidden deep in the Caves of Dare," Deirdre added, "which is where we must go."

Conchobar scratched his beard. He did not like the idea of sending his greatest warriors so far away. But if Kells was to find peace, he had no choice. "The sooner the better," the king decided. "Maeve certainly won't let what happened today go unchallenged."

Turn to page 35

While the Mystic Knights traveled to fulfill their quest, Maeve's army was on the move. With no one to stop them, the Temran soldiers were marching through Kells toward Conchobar's castle. Several villages had already been taken.

Now Torc led the army through a pine forest until they came to the next village. The Chief of Guards watched for a moment, making sure the villagers were totally unaware of their presence. Then, raising his sword, he yelled, "In the name of Queen Maeve . . . attack!"

The Temran warriors roared a war cry and attacked the people of Kells. In moments the village had been taken.

Turn to page 65

The Ice Lord raised his sword, but as he did, a great shadow fell across them all, blotting out the sun. Startled, the Evil Sentinels and the Mystic Knights all looked up.

Great wings stretched across the sky. Flames scorched the air. A voice roared like thunder.

Pyre had come.

The enormous dragon swooped across the land, letting loose fountains of flame. The three Mystic Knights could see a tiny figure riding the dragon.

"Look, it's Rohan!" Deirdre called out.

The Lightning Bat shrank back. "They've tamed the Dragon of Dare!"

Pyre dove toward the ground, shooting a stream of fire at the Evil Sentinels. The flames hit the ground and spread in all directions, scattering the four.

The Ice Lord jumped away from the flames, then glared at the Mystic Knights. "We'll take care of you later!" he swore.

His voice was filled with anger, but he could do

nothing as the dragon swerved around for another pass. The Evil Sentinels fled into the forest.

Torc hesitated. Maeve was going to be furious, and for a moment he wondered if he'd rather face the dragon instead. But as the fearsome creature swooped in for an attack, Torc ran as fast as he could back toward the Temran border.

High in the sky, Rohan watched the Temran army flee. He leaned forward, patting the great dragon's neck. "Good job, Pyre. We make a good team."

The dragon roared in agreement.

Turn to page 50

"**I** can't see them!" the Rock Wolf howled.

The Lightning Bat listened with his keen ears. "They're there, I hear them right behind the flames."

The Sea Serpent hissed in a low whisper. "I have a plan."

A moment later the firewall died down. The Mystic Knights stepped through the last of the flames, now protected by their Mystic Armor.

"Now let's finish this—" Rohan started to yell.

But the Evil Sentinels had vanished.

"Where did they go?" Ivar wondered.

Angus laughed smugly. "They knew they didn't sand a chance, so they must have run off."

Hssssss!

The Serpent's Tongue Whip burned through the air behind them. It cracked across the backs of all four heroes, throwing them off their feet.

"You're the ones who don't stand a chance!" the Sea Serpent laughed.

Stunned by the blow of the magical whip, the

Mystic Knights struggled to regain their footing as the Evil Sentinels attacked once more. The Rock Wolf loomed over Angus, snarling, "Ready to give up now?"

"I still didn't hear you say please," Angus replied.

"Please!" the Evil Sentinel howled.

"Well . . ." Angus considered. "No!"

The Mystic Knight jabbed his Terra Mace into the Rock Wolf's stomach, driving him backward into the Lightning Bat. The two Evil Sentinels stumbled away, freeing Deirdre and Angus.

"Come on!" Angus said. "Let's help the others."

"Right!" Deirdre said, turning toward Rohan and Ivar. "Maybe we can—"

She never finished her sentence. The Rock Wolf and the Lightning Bat recovered quicker than they had expected. The two Evil Sentinels sprang on her from behind, stripping away her Whirlwind Crossbow. Seeing his chance, the Ice Lord pointed his sword at her and yelled, "Give up your weapons, Mystic Knights, or your friend here is an icicle!"

"No!" Deirdre yelled, struggling against the powerful hands that held her. "Don't give up your weapons!"

The other Knights froze, uncertain what to do.

Great Seer of Tir na Nog,

the Mystic Knights need your help once again! You must decide what course of action they should take.

If you think Rohan, Angus, and Ivar should hold on to their weapons despite the danger to Deirdre, go to page 52.

If you think they should obey the Evil Sentinels and hand over their weapons, go to page 32.

Once more the Mystic Knights journeyed to the fairy ring that was the magical doorway to Tir na Nog, and once again they found themselves standing before the throne of the fairy king Fin Varra.

"Well," the powerful king said, looking at Angus, "what do we have here?"

"He accidentally wandered into a pixie field," Rohan explained.

Fin Varra laughed. "Accidentally? Are you sure? I'll bet he was thinking about his *golden* opportunity."

Deirdre stepped forward. "I implore you, King Fin Varra, do something."

Fin Varra adjusted the crown on his head. "Pixie magic, eh? Step back."

As the others moved away, the fairy king raised his scepter and pointed it at Angus. Streams of golden magic flowed from the wand and surrounded the young thief. A moment later Angus unfroze . . . right in the middle of his running stride. He continued forward and slammed right into a wall! He fell to the ground, rubbing his head and looking around in amazement.

"What happened?" he asked.

"We'll explain later, " Rohan replied.

"He's free," Fin Varra pronounced. "Now begone!"

"But King Fin Varra," Rohan said urgently, "Angus wasn't the only reason we came."

Deirdre quickly explained. "We need your help to defeat the Evil Sentinels."

"They stole our weapons—" Ivar added.

"And we still haven't tamed Pyre," Rohan interrupted.

"Stop!" the fairy king said. "Too many times you have come to Tir na Nog to ask my help. No longer will it be given."

Deirdre frowned. "But—"

"No!" Fin Varra said angrily. "I've given you the tools you need to defeat the Evil Sentinels. And when you wear the Mystic Armor, use the Dragon's Breath Daggers at your waists to summon the dragon."

A gleam of mischief filled Fin Varra's eye. "Ah, but you must tame him first. And you must defy the Evil Sentinels on your own. I can do nothing more. It's up to you."

Angus, who had just recovered from the shock of being frozen and then reawakened, managed to say, "But without your help, we will fail."

Fin Varra shrugged. "Then Kells will be lost forever."

Turn to page 54

Carried by Mider's magic, the Evil Sentinels found themselves far along the road to Conchobar's castle. The fortress could be seen in the distance. But closer, on the road before them, was an army of Temran warriors led by Torc. The Chief of Guards spotted the Evil Sentinels and rode forward. "We've taken every village between here and Temra. Now we're on to the castle. I presume you've dealt with the Mystic Knights?"

"They tricked us and got away," the Ice Lord admitted. "We're looking for them!"

"You won't have to look far!"

Deirdre, Angus, and Ivar stepped onto the road, putting themselves between the castle and the invading army.

The Temran warriors stopped in their tracks. Many of them had fought the Mystic Knights before and lost. Some dropped their weapons. Others started to back away.

"The Mystic Knights!" a Temran shouted. "Run!"

The nervous Temrans turned and fled, stumbling over one another in the effort to escape the powerful heroes.

"Get back here, you cowards!" Torc roared. "Take care of this lot!" But the Temran soldiers feared the Mystic Knights more than they feared Torc, and they kept running.

The Rock Wolf laughed. "Don't worry. We won't need them."

Torc glanced at the heroes. "It does appear that one Knight is still missing."

"And soon they'll all be missing!" the Ice Lord promised. He drew his Black Ice Sword and the other Evil Sentinels raised their own weapons.

As they started forward, the three Mystic Knights retreated a few steps. After Rohan had vanished behind the wall of flame, they knew there was nothing they could do to help. Either his plan would work or he would be defeated. Either way, their next step was clear—they had to return to Conchobar's castle to defend it from the invading Temran army. They'd had no idea, though, that the Evil Sentinels had found a way to break the pixie spell.

"I know coming back here was the right thing to do," Angus said. "But I wish we could use our weapons."

Deirdre blinked. "By all the castles in Kells, we can!" She drew her Whirlwind Crossbow and fired. A mighty whirlwind shot from the weapon, causing the Evil Sentinels to scatter.

"Don't you see?" She laughed. "Our weapons

were frozen with the Evil Sentinels. Now that they're unfrozen, our weapons are, too!"

Angus and Ivar raised the Terra Mace and the Barbed Trident. "Fire!" Deirdre shouted. The three Knights unleashed their magic once again.

But the Evil Sentinels did not fear the Mystic Knights the way the common soldiers did. They released the power of their own weapons, and the two separate blasts met each other halfway, canceling each other out. The Mystic Knights and the Evil Sentinels then charged into hand-to-hand combat.

Deirdre kicked the Rock Wolf, knocking him into the Sea Serpent. Angus brought his Terra Mace crashing down on the Ice Lord, while Ivar jabbed with the Barbed Trident, driving the Lightning Bat off balance.

The sudden strength of the Knights' attack had caught the Evil Sentinels off guard. But they were strong, and they outnumbered the heroes. They quickly gathered themselves for another charge.

"Their powers are too great!" Ivar warned.

"It's not like we have a lot of options!" Angus countered.

Before Ivar could reply, the Evil Sentinels were on top of them. The Rock Wolf's eyes flashed, and a beam of magical light shot forward, catching Angus in the chest. The blow sent him flying backward.

Now the four Evil Sentinels surrounded Deirdre and Ivar.

The Rock Wolf and the Lightning Bat grabbed Deirdre as the Sea Serpent lashed Ivar with lightning bolts from his whip, throwing him off his feet.

The Ice Lord stepped forward, pointing his sword at the three Mystic Knights. "It's over, foolish heroes. Give up."

Nearby, Torc looked on eagerly. "Finish them off," he urged. "Finish them!"

Turn to page 21

Rohan dropped the Sword of Kells.

Reluctantly, Angus and Ivar followed his example, dropping their weapons next to his.

Hissing in delight, the Sea Serpent scooped up the weapons.

As the Evil Sentinels howled in delight, Deirdre saw her chance. Lashing out, she kicked Lightning Bat in the chest, then whirled around and slammed Rock Wolf in the stomach. Ducking under the grasp of the other two Evil Sentinels, she scrambled toward freedom and rejoined her friends.

The four Evil Sentinels quickly recovered. Armed with their own weapons and those of the Mystic Knights, they started forward. "This is the end for you," Ice Lord said in a low, cold voice.

"Uh-oh," Angus said, looking down at his weaponless hands.

"I never thought I would say this," Ivar urged, "but we have to retreat!"

"No," Rohan muttered.

Deirdre grabbed his arm as the Evil Sentinels stalked forward. "Rohan, we have no choice!"

The Evil Sentinels broke into a run, ready to crush the Mystic Knights once and for all. Finally, Rohan turned, and with the others, he fled down the hill. His face turned red with shame as he heard the Evil Sentinels let out a cry of victory.

Turn to page 43

Temran warriors swept through another village, sending the innocent villagers running for their lives. For a moment Torc thought he would meet no resistance at all as his army captured more Kells territory. But as his men began to ransack the small town, a battalion of Kells soldiers arrived.

Maeve's Chief of Guards laughed. "Those Kellsmen don't stand a chance!"

The Kells soldiers charged. Torc and his men leaped forward to meet the attack. The Chief of Guards was the first to cross swords with Conchobar's troops as a young Kellsman stabbed at him. Torc easily dodged the blow and knocked the other warrior to the ground.

One of the Temran warriors turned to Torc and laughed. "Without the Mystic Knights to help them, they're like babes in arms!"

Torc nodded. "We don't have to worry about those Mystic Knights . . . unless the Evil Sentinels are sleeping on the job."

Turn to page 57

Even as Conchobar spoke, miles away Queen Maeve sat on her throne and listened to Torc describe his defeat at the hands of the Mystic Knights.

"We had victory within our grasp!" Torc fumed. "Then those four imps interfered!"

Maeve thought silently for a moment. "I assume they used their weapons?"

"Of course," Torc replied. "Otherwise we would never have been defeated."

Maeve rose from her seat. Her black robes swirled around her as she paced through the gloom of her throne room. "In order to bring Kells to its knees, the Mystic Knights must be eliminated." She stopped, struck with a realization. "Why, of course! The Evil Sentinels!"

Torc shrugged. "What about them? They've already been defeated."

"Individually, yes," Maeve said. "But together, united as my own personal guards, they would be unstoppable."

Torc considered her plan. "A brilliant thought, my

queen . . . but how will you get them to do your bidding?"

Maeve smiled evilly. "I'll just use my charm on Mider."

"Your charm is wearing thin," spoke a voice from behind the Evil Queen.

Maeve whirled around. Above a chalice in the center of the room, the air burst into green flame. Out of the flame stepped Mider. The dark fairy was tiny, with black hair and pointy teeth, and evil power radiated from him in potent waves.

"Mider," the queen cooed. "I didn't know you were there."

"Of course you didn't," the fairy replied.

"I need to make a request of you," Maeve said.

"You dare!" Mider snapped. "You dare make another request of me! It was your mishandling of the rune stone I gave you that led to the defeat of my Four Sentinels."

Maeve scowled. "Me? My so-called 'mishandling' was—"

"Silence!" the dark fairy roared. The green flames around him shot up until they scorched the roof of Maeve's throne room . . . and Mider grew with the flames, until he loomed over Maeve. "You will return the rune stone to Mider. Now!"

The Evil Queen stepped back from the suddenly tall Mider, surrounded by magic flame. She clutched her scepter and the magic stone that glowed at its tip. Maeve could not afford to make Mider angry. The powerful dark fairy had always been her ally, but he had his own mysterious reasons for wanting to destroy Kells. If she made him angry enough, he might leave her for good and find new allies to help him with his schemes.

"Mider," Maeve pleaded, "I implore you to give me another chance." She smiled. "I have a plan for the final defeat of Kells and those irksome Mystic Knights."

The green flames shrank back to their smaller size and Mider dwindled along with them. "Tell me of your plan," Mider said.

"I will unite the Four Sentinels of Temra," Maeve explained, "and have them fight as a single unconquerable force."

Mider looked pleased. Without another word, he began to summon the Evil Sentinels by calling out their names.

"Rath Coghan, the Ice Lord!" At Mider's command, a grim figure appeared. His armor looked like it had been carved out of bones, and his face was that of a skeleton. In his hands he held a wicked blade called the Black Ice Sword.

"Bane Morfan, the Rock Wolf!" Mider shouted. A second armored figure appeared, looking more like a wolf than a man. On his right arm, he wore a fanglike weapon called the Wolf's Tooth Claw.

"Forgal Mac Roig, the Sea Serpent!" The third Evil Sentinel appeared, just as monstrous as the first two: a reptile in the shape of a man. He cracked his weapon: the Serpent's Tongue Whip.

"Sonarus Skye," Mider chanted, "the Lightning Bat!" The last Sentinel appeared, his batlike face glaring at everyone in the throne room. He wielded a strange and deadly sharp boomerang device called the Bat-el-Axe.

Together, the Four Sentinels looked so fierce that even Maeve and Torc took a step backward. But Maeve quickly hid her fear.

"Perhaps we should test them," she suggested.

Mider waved his hand. Instantly, four ghostly spirits appeared. Screaming like banshees, the spirits attacked.

The startled Evil Sentinels were knocked off balance. But it only took them a moment to recover . . . and to prepare to fight.

One by one each Evil Sentinel raised his weapon in the air.

"Try my Black Ice Sword!" Rath Coghan yelled.

"Sample my Wolf's Tooth Claw!" Bane Morfan growled.

"Feel the sting of my Serpent's Tongue Whip!" hissed Forgal Mac Roig.

"And to finish it off, I'll use my Bat-el-Axe!" screeched Sonarus Skye.

Attacking together, the fierce Evil Sentinels struck back at the spirits Mider had summoned. Their magic weapons lashed out, and in seconds the spirits were turned to dust.

Maeve let out an evil laugh that echoed off the walls in her throne room. "The end has come for Kells and the Mystic Knights!" she declared.

Turn to page 44

A vast army of Temran warriors scurried about Maeve's castle, swarming like ants. As the Evil Queen looked on, Torc walked among the troops, making sure they were ready for battle. When he was satisfied, he returned to Maeve's side.

"The battalion is now ready to attack Kells," he growled.

"Splendid," Maeve said. "Don't worry about those Mystic Knights interfering. The Evil Sentinels will take care of them."

A wicked smile twisted its way across Torc's lips. "And victory shall be ours."

As hordes of Temran soldiers prepared to march toward the border, the Mystic Knights sat together in a corner of Conchobar's courtyard, thinking about the mysterious riddle Fin Varra had given them. The heroes had been joined by Aideen, a tiny, cute fairy who had often helped them in the past. She fluttered about their heads as they talked.

"It's got to have something to do with the shell," Rohan suggested. "Our Mystic Armor acts like the turtle's shell."

Ivar nodded. "Agreed."

"No, no," Deirdre argued. "It's *Pyre's* shell. Don't you see, his cave acts like his shell. We've got to keep him in his cave."

"His cave!" Ivar grunted doubtfully.

"He was in his cave and we still couldn't even slow him down," Rohan reminded her.

"Maybe the turtles are a distraction," Angus said. "When I was a pickpocket, I used to . . ." Angus suddenly realized that he probably shouldn't bring up his former profession as a thief. "Um . . . well . . . never mind."

Aideen fluttered down to the ground. "Perhaps it would help if we observed turtles." The fairy sprinkled magic powder on the ground. Instantly, four small pebbles transformed into four slow-moving turtles.

"How darling," Deirdre said. "Do they bite?"

"No," Aideen answered.

Deirdre reached down to pet one of the turtles. As she did, it snapped at her, nearly taking one of her fingers off. She glared at Aideen.

Aideen shrugged. "Or maybe they do."

"Enough of these shell games," spoke a voice above them. Cathbad the Druid was standing over them, looking down at the four turtles. He plucked a vial from his pouch and cast a cloud of his own magic powder over the turtles. Without a sound, they changed back into pebbles.

"What's going on here?" Cathbad asked. "I thought

you were supposed to be taming Pyre."

"We're trying, Cathbad," Rohan said. "The only clue Fin Varra gave us was a turtle."

"So we're watching turtles, trying to figure out what he meant," Ivar added.

Cathbad stroked his beard thoughtfully. "Rather than observe a turtle, think like one. What does a turtle do while under attack?"

Deirdre shrugged. "A turtle doesn't do anything."

"Aye, that's it!" Rohan shouted, leaping to his feet. "The turtle never actually defeats its opponents. It just hides in its shell and allows its enemies to wear themselves out."

Cathbad tapped Rohan on the forehead. "Now you're thinking."

Ivar stood up. "So what are we waiting for? We've got a vicious dragon to tame!"

At that moment, King Conchobar rushed out of the palace with two soldiers at his back. "Raise the gates! Assemble my battalions!" he roared.

"Father, what is it?" Deirdre asked.

Conchobar stopped. "I just received a message that Maeve's forces are massing on the border. We have precious little time."

"Maeve's on her way here?" Rohan asked. "Should we join the army?"

"I'm not sure that is a wise idea," Cathbad said. "Your task is to tame Pyre and summon the warrior Draganta."

"But how can we leave when there's a battle to be fought?" Ivar asked. "What should we do?"

O Great Seer!

Your wisdom is needed now.

If you think the Mystic Knights should march out to face Maeve's army immediately, go to page 78.

If you think they should continue their quest to tame Pyre first, go to page 5.

On the northern border of Kells, that same victory cry was echoed by the Temran soldiers. The invading army watched as the army of Kells turned and ran, defeated by Maeve's soldiers.

Torc howled in delight. "Ha! Look at them run! We are victorious!"

The Chief of Guards rode like a foul wind back to Maeve's castle to deliver the good news. He arrived just as the Evil Sentinels reached the fortress, and together they delivered their reports: the Kellsmen had been defeated, and the Mystic Knights had been stripped of their weapons.

On her dark throne, Maeve cackled with glee. "Now my birthright shall finally be fulfilled—I shall rule the entire island!"

Her horrible, chilling laugh seemed to echo for miles.

Turn to page 70

As Maeve and Mider plotted, the Mystic Knights marched toward the far border of Kells. High in the mountains of the north lay the Caves of Dare, where the great dragon Pyre made his lair. Rohan and the others traveled hard and fast until they reached the mountains, then made their way up a narrow, winding trail.

"Why . . . why do these caves have to be so far away?" Angus gasped.

Rohan looked up at the mountain looming over them. He could see the opening to the caves up ahead. "We're here."

Angus sat down. "Well, I've got to rest before facing that dragon."

Ivar shook his head. "This is your third rest, Angus!"

Angus scowled and picked up a pebble. He jokingly tossed it at Ivar, but the other Knight ducked. The pebble sailed over Ivar's helmet and hit Deirdre on the head.

She whirled around. "Why you . . . !"

Angus raised his hands. "It was an accident. Honest!"

Deirdre glared. "An accident, was it?"

Angus backed away as Deirdre stalked toward him. "If I'm lying, may a bolt of fire hit me from the sky—"

Without warning, a stream of fire roared down from above and struck the ground behind Angus, lighting his pants on fire. "Yow!" he yelled. He jumped forward and nearly landed in Deirdre's arms. Angus patted the seat of his pants until the flames smoldered out.

"It came from the cave," Rohan said. They all looked up, just as the great dragon stuck its head and long neck out of the cave entrance. When he opened his mouth, Pyre could have swallowed all four of them at once. When he roared, the sky itself seemed to tremble.

"Looks like Pyre has a warm welcome for us," Ivar said.

Turn to page 10

Rohan spoke bravely, but words alone could not stop Maeve and her powerful army. The next day, as Conchobar gathered the last of his forces to defend his kingdom, a messenger staggered into the palace. His clothes were tattered and he was covered in dust and mud from days of hard travel. Exhausted, he fell to the ground at Conchobar's feet. "Temra!" he gasped. "Temran soldiers have taken the northern border!"

Deirdre, who had been sitting at her father's side, leaped to her feet. "There's no time left, we must find Draganta now!"

"Before we can find Draganta," Ivar said, "we must tame the dragon Pyre."

Angus shook his head. "The Evil Sentinels have our weapons, maybe we should ask them to tame Pyre."

Rohan slowly stood up, his jaw set in determination. "We'll go to Tir na Nog and ask Fin Varra to help us."

The Mystic Knights set out from Conchobar's castle and headed for the fairy ring in the Boyne Valley that would transport them to the magical kingdom of Tir na Nog. They had not gone far, though, before they passed a beautiful field covered in wildflowers. Angus, sharp-eyed as usual, spotted something shining in the middle of the clearing.

"There's gold in that field," he said, stopping suddenly.

The others glanced into the open space. "I don't see anything," Ivar said.

Rohan laughed. "Trust him," he told Ivar. "Angus can spot a speck of gold in a dust storm."

"And he can tell if you've got gold fillings without even seeing you smile," Deirdre added. "But we don't have time for that now, Angus. We've got to get to Tir na Nog."

Angus laughed. "I won't be but a heartbeat!"

He jogged toward the field, barely noticing that the edge of the wildflower patch was surrounded by small piles of stones. He hurried past them and ran into the middle of the field.

And froze.

The others blinked. They couldn't believe their eyes. Angus stood as still as a statue in the middle of the clearing, frozen right in the middle of a step.

"What happened?" Ivar asked.

"I don't know," Rohan said, "but he needs our help. Let's go!"

"No!" a small voice cried.

The three heroes pulled up short as the fairy Aideen appeared before them. "Stop! Can't you see the markers? It's a pixie field!" She pointed to the small piles of stones at the edge of the clearing.

"What's a pixie field?" Rohan asked.

The fairy fluttered her wings. "Mischievous pixies set them up for their own amusement. Whoever steps onto one freezes in their tracks."

"Forever?" Deirdre asked.

"At least," Aideen replied. "Unless you can get Fin Varra to help. But Fin Varra would never leave Tir na Nog to come here for so small a task."

"No problem," Ivar said as he pulled a rope from his pack. "We'll just bring the task to him." With a quick knot, Ivar turned the rope into a lasso. He swung it over his head a few times, then let go. The looped end of the lasso landed around Angus's waist.

"Now pull!" Ivar instructed the others.

The three heroes dragged Angus from the field. But even as he was dragged through the flowers, the Knight did not move a muscle. Once Angus was clear of the pixie field, the others raised him to his feet again. Moving him was like moving a stone statue. They called his name, trying to wake him, but it was useless.

"Angus!" Deirdre said, slapping him across the face. She got no reaction.

"Angus!" Ivar cried, slapping him again.

"I already tried that," Deirdre said.

Ivar grinned. "I know. But I always wanted to do that anyway."

Turn to page 26

Cheers rose up from the walls of Conchobar's castle as the Mystic Knights passed through the gates. Once the Temrans had been routed, Rohan released Pyre to return to his cave. Then he joined his friends.

As they entered the courtyard, King Conchobar came out to meet them, embracing his daughter and shaking the hands of the three other Knights. Amid the cheers of the Kellsmen, the heroes told Conchobar all that had happened.

"We thought Rohan was done for," Deirdre said as they described the final battle with Pyre.

"Well done, in fact!" Angus added with a laugh.

"But he finally wore Pyre down and was able to tame him," Ivar reported.

Conchobar shook his head. The expression on his face was a mixture of joy and disbelief. "Is the dragon really tame?"

Deirdre nodded. "Pyre still has a strong will of his own. But he will come when summoned by our Dragon's Breath Daggers."

Rohan smiled. "Let's make sure."

The young hero drew a dagger from the belt of his Mystic Armor. Holding it high, he pressed a jewel on the handle. Blue streaks of magic crackled in the air . . . followed by a great roar that echoed throughout the land.

Pyre had answered the call. From now on Kells would live under his protection.

And the protection of the Mystic Knights of Tir na Nog!

The saga of the Mystic Knights
continues in Book #5,
DRAGANTA REVEALED!

Don't miss the magic!

52

"**A** strong warrior never surrenders his weapons," Ivar declared.

"Ivar's right!" Deirdre called out.

"Attack!" Rohan shouted.

Rohan raised the Sword of Kells and was about to send a blast of fire at the Rock Wolf, but the Evil Sentinel used Deirdre as a shield, and Rohan was forced to extinguish his flame.

Ivar aimed his Barbed Trident at the Sea Serpent, but the slippery creature dove behind the others. Ivar had to hold his fire, or his lightning strike would have blasted Deirdre.

"This calls for something up close and personal," Angus declared. He charged up to the Evil Sentinels and swung his Terra Mace, trying to hurl the fearsome warriors away from Deirdre. But the Evil Sentinels were too quick. Just before the mace could strike them, they pulled Deirdre into its path. The mace crashed against Deirdre's Mystic Armor with a sound like thunder.

The blow knocked the wind out of Deirdre, but the ear-splitting noise also shook the Evil Sentinels off their feet. "This is our chance!" Rohan cried, springing forward.

He was just about to grab Deirdre and pull her away from the Rock Wolf's grip when the Sea Serpent snapped his Serpent's Tongue Whip. The whip wrapped itself around Rohan's legs, pulling him off his feet. Ivar, close behind Rohan, tumbled over the other Knight and fell forward. He rolled up smoothly onto his feet, only to receive a kick in the stomach from the Ice Lord.

Rohan, Angus, and Ivar staggered backward as the Evil Sentinels jeered at them. "Now do you see!" the Ice Lord laughed. "Give up your weapons or I'll freeze her where she stands!"

Deirdre, still stunned from Angus's blow, managed to gasp, "No . . . never give up your weapons."

Rohan hesitated. Maybe Deirdre was wrong. Perhaps Ivar had been wrong, too. Perhaps there were times when even a true warrior surrendered his weapons.

Turn to page 32

The Mystic Knights returned to Kells with heavy hearts. They were supposed to be the heroes who saved the day. Instead they felt like failures.

In Conchobar's castle the Knights, along with the fairy Aideen, who had traveled with them, found Cathbad the Druid waiting for them. One look at their faces told the druid everything he needed to know.

Rohan shook his head. "We've lost our weapons, and we can't tame Pyre, so we'll never find Draganta. And now Fin Varra refuses to help us."

Cathbad nodded. "Yes, things look bad, my lad. It's true you're weakened without your weapons, but it is sometimes cunning and not strength that leads one to victory."

Ivar snorted. "Any thoughts on how we can be cunning enough to get our weapons back?"

The druid's only reply was mysterious. "That is for the four of you to figure out." Then, with a swirl of his cloak, the druid departed.

Angus scowled. "Why are the wise men always the hardest ones to understand?"

"That wasn't so hard," Deirdre said. "He means we have to solve this problem on our own."

"I've got it!" Rohan cried. "We were able to defeat the Evil Sentinels when they were separate."

"But how do we separate that pack of wolves?" Deirdre asked.

"And you forget, we had our weapons back then," Ivar pointed out.

"Well, I didn't say the plan was perfect," Rohan admitted.

Aideen piped up. "I know! I know!"

"Not now, Aideen," Rohan said. "We're trying to come up with a plan."

"But I've got a plan!" Aideen squeaked. "A good plan!"

Ivar ignored her. "If we could only figure out a way to disarm them."

"But—" Aideen tried again.

"Perhaps if we attacked under cover of night?" Deirdre suggested.

"Listen to me!" Aideen screeched as the Mystic Knights continued to talk.

Turn the page

Great
Seer of
Tir na Nog,
the four heroes need
your wisdom once more.

Should the Mystic Knights
try to create a plan of their
own?
If so, then go to page 61.

Should the heroes listen to
Aideen?
If so, go to page 75.

Torc could not know how right he was. Miles away the Evil Sentinels were still frozen in the pixie field. They might have remained there for years, but Mider wondered what was taking so long and had gone out to find them.

"A pixie field!" the dark fairy said angrily. "How dare anyone cast spells over my Evil Sentinels!"

With a wave of his hand, the dark fairy broke the spell. The Evil Sentinels stumbled out of the field and fell at Mider's feet.

The Ice Lord was the first to rise. "Those Mystic Knights tricked us!"

Mider nodded. "Then go. Take your revenge on them now!"

With another wave of his hand, Mider sent the Evil Sentinels into one final battle for control of Kells.

Turn to page 28

58

Pyre blasted more smoke and flames at the Mystic Knights, and their choice seemed obvious now. The Mystic Knights turned and ran, with flames licking at their heels.

Rohan and the others hurried toward a fairy ring they had discovered on an earlier adventure. At the center of the ring stood a dolman—an ancient stone monument—with a crystal in the middle of the capstone. As all four Mystic Knights touched this stone together, they were engulfed in a flash of white light.

When their eyes were no longer dazzled, the heroes found themselves in the throne room of Fin Varra, king of the fairies and ruler of Tir na Nog. The throne room was an enormous, gloomy cavern, with torches flickering against the surrounding cave walls. In the middle of the room was a court filled with the bustling activity of dozens of wee folk. Some of the little people were ugly and twisted, some looked exactly like humans—only much smaller, and some were beautiful, with glowing eyes and rainbow wings.

In the center of the court was Fin Varra's throne.

The fairy king did not seem surprised to see the Mystic Knights when they appeared in front of him. But then, he had great magic power at his command, and always seemed to know what the heroes were thinking before they asked.

Fin Varra listened patiently as Rohan described their recent effort to tame the great dragon. The others stood behind Rohan, nodding in agreement . . . except for Angus, who had caught the eye of a beautiful, shimmering fairy woman standing off to one side. He cast a sly smile in her direction.

"We followed the rules," Rohan was saying. "We obtained the Mystic Armor, and now when we try to tame Pyre, we can't." Rohan stared hard at the fairy king. "So what is it you're not telling us?"

Fin Varra shook his head. "You should blame no one but yourself for failure."

Angus glanced away from the beautiful fairy woman. "Well, you try taming that scaly-skinned fireball!" he replied to Fin Varra, and then gave the beautiful fairy a wink. She winked back, and Angus felt his heart pound faster.

"Aren't you as pretty as the dew on a morning flower," he told her.

The fairy woman smiled sweetly. But suddenly her smile seemed to widen, twisting her face into a gruesome mess of flesh. Before Angus could react, the beautiful fairy turned into a disgusting Spriggan—the most foul, twisted, and nasty type of wee folk. "Why, thank you!" The Spriggan belched as it spit black goo onto Angus.

"Yuck!" Angus muttered to himself, wiping goo out

of his eyes. "Not even Mystic Armor can defend me against that!"

The others were too intent on Fin Varra to notice Angus's mischief. They listened as the fairy king said, "I never told you that taming the dragon would be simple."

"I've tamed the wildest horses in Kells, and toppled wild boars since I was knee-high!" Rohan scoffed.

Ivar puffed out his chest. "And I, single-handedly, have trained tigers in distant lands."

Fin Varra chuckled. "Pyre is not like any other animal. You cannot tame him like any other animal."

Deirdre stepped forward. "So what are we supposed to do?"

Fin Varra waved his jeweled scepter over a pool of water built into the armrest of his throne. "Look into the reflecting pool," he instructed.

The water bubbled for a moment before becoming perfectly smooth. An image of a giant sea turtle appeared.

"Behold the simple turtle," Fin Varra said. "The slowest animal on earth fears no one, for it knows how to battle all enemies."

Angus wiped a little more goo from his mouth. "And so . . . ?"

Fin Varra shrugged. "That is all."

Rohan waited for Fin Varra to explain, but the fairy king met his gaze with silence. The young hero realized that the mysterious riddle was all the help they would get.

Turn to page 39

61

Rohan shushed Aideen by pressing his finger to his own lips. "I still think trying to separate them is the best idea. It's our only chance to get our weapons back."

The others agreed. Without hesitating, they started out to challenge the Evil Sentinels once more.

Since Maeve had already captured the northern border, the Mystic Knights knew exactly where to go. They headed north on the main road, and before long they came to a forest in northern Kells. Reminders of a recently fought battle were everywhere. Broken swords and spears lay scattered on the ground, and the flags and banners of Kells battalions had been trampled into the mud.

"This must have been a terrible battle," Deirdre whispered sadly.

"Not nearly as terrible as the one you're about to fight!" sneered a cold, familiar voice.

The Ice Lord stepped out of the shadows of a large tree.

"Prepare to meet your doom!" howled the Rock Wolf, appearing from the other side of the road. Then the Sea Serpent appeared in front of the Mystic Knights, and the Lightning Bat swooped in from behind. Each of the four Evil Sentinels had his own weapon—and one of the weapons taken from the Mystic Knights.

"Remember the plan," Rohan whispered to the others. Then, out loud, he shouted, "Ho there, Ice Lord! That Black Ice Sword has frozen your brain if you think you can ever defeat me. Remember, I've already beaten you once!"

The Ice Lord spoke in a voice like crunching ice. "I'll freeze you and use you as an ice sculpture in my home before we're through, Kellsman!"

"Then prove it!" Rohan challenged. He turned and plunged into the forest, daring the Ice Lord to stop him.

Rohan ran as swiftly as he could, dodging around trees, slipping under branches, and jumping over huge tree roots. He heard heavy footsteps behind him and knew that the Ice Lord was following closely.

Not far off Rohan spotted a large, bare clearing that the Knights had noticed on their last visit northward. Rohan sprinted for it, breaking through the trees and onto the barren ground. Then he turned and waited.

The Ice Lord burst out of the forest behind him, snapping branches as though they were twigs. He held the Black Ice Sword in his right hand and the Sword of Kells in his left.

"Now, you little upstart," the Evil Sentinel said. "Who is afraid of whom?"

Rohan smiled. "I am afraid of one thing. I'm afraid you've fallen into a trap!"

At his words, Deirdre, Angus, and Ivar stepped out of the trees, surrounding the Ice Lord. Alone, none of them were a match for the Evil Sentinel and his magical weapons. But together they believed they should be able to withstand his assaults.

But when he saw the four Knights, the Ice Lord only laughed.

"Surrender, Ice Lord!" Rohan demanded.

"Ridiculous!" the Evil Sentinel said. "Do you think I'd fall for such a simple trap?"

"You did fall for it." Rohan grinned. "We wanted to separate you from the others. Now you're alone."

The Ice Lord said in mocking voice, "Who said I was alone?"

As he spoke, the three other Evil Sentinels appeared and attacked without warning.

The Mystic Knights barely turned in time to defend themselves. Soon the forest rang with the sounds of battle.

Still holding both his own Black Ice Sword and Rohan's Sword of Kells, the Ice Lord laughed. "You thought you'd try to separate us? Why would we want to break up our little group, now that we fight so well together?"

Rohan stumbled backward. Without a weapon there was no way he could defeat the Ice Lord. "Fall back!" he called to his friends.

The other Mystic Knights were already retreating. They turned their backs on the Evil Sentinels and ran as lightning bolts and whirlwinds battered the trees behind them. They ran until the sounds of evil laughter faded.

"Well," Angus gasped when they finally stopped. "That didn't work."

Ivar looked at Rohan. "What do we do now?"

Turn to page 75

Not far from the cave mouth, Rohan signaled for the others to stop.

"Do you see him anywhere?" Angus asked.

Rohan shook his head. "No, but I feel him."

Ivar kicked something at his feet. It was a large bone, still charred and smoking from dragon's fire. "Looks like something else felt him, too. And not too long ago."

Rohan gulped. "We'd better prepare." He straightened up and called out, "Fire within me!" In a flash of brilliantly colored light, he was surrounded by the Mystic Armor of Fire. Next the hills echoed with three more cries.

"Earth beneath me!"

"Air above me!"

"Water around me!"

The air crackled with mystical power as the other three Knights summoned their armor. Knowing they had no time to waste, Rohan strode up to the cave. Inside, all was dark. He boomed, "Pyre, show yourself and be tamed!"

He was answered by silence.

Deirdre stepped up beside him. "Then we're coming to get you!"

With the speed and strength of a storm, the dragon burst out of the darkness. His roar was like thunder. His fire was stronger than lightning. His footsteps shook the earth, and his wings beat the air into a great wind.

Before he even reached them, the Mystic Knights were knocked off their feet.

"Maybe we should use our weapons!" Angus shouted over all the noise.

"Not yet," Rohan said. "Take cover!" He led them behind a large boulder.

"Now?" Angus asked.

"Not yet!" Rohan insisted.

Angus waited just a second before asking, "How about now?"

Rohan peered out behind the boulder. The dragon was almost upon them. "Okay. Now!"

The Mystic Knights leaped out from behind their cover, pointed their weapons at the dragon . . . and fired!

But nothing happened.

Ivar shook his Barbed Trident. "What in the name of the Seven Seas is going on?"

Deirdre looked at her Whirlwind Crossbow. "Our weapons must still be frozen from the pixie field!"

"Which means we're pretty defenseless!" Angus yelled.

The dragon loomed over them.

"Roll!" Rohan yelled. The Mystic Knights dove out

of the way, rolling to safety as the dragon brought one massive claw down, crushing the boulder where they had hidden.

"In here!" Ivar called out. He had rolled right up to a large crevice in the hillside, large enough for all the Knights to fit in but too small for Pyre's claws and fangs. The heroes scrambled inside as a fireball exploded against the hillside nearby, charring the gray stone black.

Inside the crevice, Deirdre punched her fist in frustration. "How are we supposed to defeat Pyre with our weapons still frozen?"

"I don't know, but we can't stay here long," Angus said, looking at their hiding place. "Pyre will get in here sooner or later. I feel like a turtle without his shell."

Angus's words echoed in Rohan's head. *A turtle without his shell . . .*

"That's it!" Rohan cried.

"What?" Angus asked.

Rohan turned to the others. "Don't you remember? Fin Varra and the story of the turtle."

Ivar realized what Rohan meant. "That's right. When a turtle's attacked, it doesn't fight back. It retreats into its shell until the attacker wears itself out."

Deirdre, too, caught on. "If we're right about this, we have to get Pyre to wear himself out."

"But if we're wrong," Angus pointed out, "we won't be able to defend ourselves and that dragon will crush us." He peered nervously out of the crevice, eyeing the dragon, which snorted and growled, searching for them. "I say we go back to Fin Varra and ask him to remove the spell from our weapons."

Rohan hesitated, considering Angus's suggestion.

Great Seer of Tir na Nog,

you have guided the Mystic Knights well thus far. Now they need your help again!

If you believe the Mystic Knights should go to Fin Varra for help, go to page 71.

If you believe the heroes should try to tame Pyre right away, go to page 7.

Miles away, a dark cloud hung over Conchobar's palace. His soldiers had been scattered, and the Mystic Knights had lost a terrible battle. The four heroes stood before King Conchobar battered and bruised.

Cathbad the Druid put a hand on Rohan's shoulder. "It's better to retreat and fight another day, my lad."

The king grunted. "But the next battle cannot end in failure, for all of Kells will then surely be lost."

Ivar slammed one fist into the other hand. "We need Pyre—we'll have to face him without our weapons!"

"And face the Evil Sentinels, too," Deirdre reminded him.

"We'll do both," Rohan said. "And we'll succeed. We'll never surrender!"

Turn to page 46

Deirdre nodded. "Angus may be right. Without our weapons, there's no way we can withstand that dragon, let alone tame him."

Reluctantly, Rohan nodded. "Let's get to Tir na Nog."

The Knights scrambled out of their crevice and ran. Pyre beat his great wings, stirring up a wind that practically lifted them off their feet and carried them down the mountainside.

At the bottom of the hill, the Mystic Knights dusted themselves off and started toward the fairy ring in the Boyne Valley.

Little did they know that they were being watched by a pair of unfriendly eyes. Mider the dark fairy had transported himself to northern Kells in search of the missing Evil Sentinels. Hearing the dragon's roar, he had come to investigate, and spotted the four Mystic Knights hurrying away from the Caves of Dare.

"Pyre is too much for them," the dark fairy laughed to himself. "They're probably journeying to get some help from that accursed meddler, Fin Varra. Well, my foolish heroes, if it's a journey you want, it's a journey you'll get!"

Calling up an evil spell, Mider cast his magic across the forest.

The Mystic Knights never saw Mider, but soon they sensed a sudden change in the forest. The shadows under the trees grew longer and darker. The path they had been taking twisted and turned.

"You know, I don't remember the path being this tangled," Ivar said.

Angus shrugged. "I can never tell. All forests look the same to me."

"And that's another thing, " Ivar continued. "I feel like we've passed by this spot already."

Rohan looked around. "How can that be? We've been following the same path."

"Maybe," Deirdre said, "but Ivar's right. I recognize this tree. Last time I saw it, I thought how those two branches looked like huge hands." She kicked the bark of a nearby tree with two big limbs that hung low, like the arms of a giant.

The Knights walked farther, but with every step, the darkness grew. The trees seemed to press in close around them. After another few minutes of walking, Deirdre called out, "By the magic of the fairies! It is the same tree!"

"Are you sure?" Rohan asked. "That would mean we've been walking in circles."

"I'm sure." She walked over and kicked the tree again.

The other knights could hardly believed their eyes as the two branches that looked like arms reached down and wrapped themselves around Deirdre, then lifted her easily into the air.

"Help!" Deirdre cried.

The others rushed forward, but Deirdre had been raised too high to reach. She felt the tree's great branches start to squeeze her. "Aggh!" she cried. "It's crushing me!"

"We've got to get her down!" Rohan yelled.

"Rohan, look out!" Ivar warned.

Rohan ducked, and the branches of another tree grabbed only the air.

Angus looked around. In every direction, he could see trees coming to life, reaching out for them with their huge branches. As the branches moved, the leaves rubbed together, filling the forest with an angry-sounding hiss. "This is not—" Angus began.

His words were cut off as a tree behind him wrapped its limbs around his chest, squeezing the air out of him.

Ivar jumped away from the grasp of another tree-monster. But the trees were everywhere, and he stepped right into the clutches of still another.

Rohan dodged away from yet another enchanted tree. The tree-monsters were impossible to avoid. Every branch was like an arm with dozens of hands and fingers grasping and clawing at him. He heard the others crying for help, but he found himself pinned down by a swarm of branches and he could do nothing.

Desperately, Rohan raised the Sword of Kells. He summoned its magic fire.

Instantly, the trees pulled back. The branches

seemed to shiver, and the hiss of the leaves, which before had sounded like anger, now sounded like fear.

"Rohan, that's it!" Angus called out. "The trees are afraid of the fire!"

"Back! Back!" Rohan said, jabbing his flaming sword at more trees. Their branches withdrew, giving him space. Rohan rushed to Deirdre's tree and held the sword close to the bark. "Let her go!"

The tree seemed to understand. Quick as a summer storm, it lowered Deirdre to the ground, then lifted its branches high to avoid the flames. Rohan then rushed to the trees that held Ivar and Angus, and those tree-monsters also gave up their prisoners.

"Let's get out of here," Rohan suggested.

Holding the Sword of Kells high to keep the tree-monsters away, he led them forward along the path.

Perhaps it was the light of the flaming sword, or perhaps it was because the tree-monsters no longer tried to confuse them, but now their path went straight and true through the forest. In a few minutes they emerged from the trees . . . only to find themselves back at the Caves of Dare! Spotting them, Pyre roared out a challenge.

"We're . . . we're right back where we started," Ivar said in disbelief.

"It must have been some kind of spell," Deirdre guessed. "We've done nothing but waste time."

Angus looked up at the caves, then back at the forest. "Should we risk the forest again, or go back and face the dragon?"

Turn to page 7

75

The four Evil Sentinels stomped through the forest. They were eager for another fight with the Mystic Knights, sure that this time they would defeat the heroes forever.

The Rock Wolf sniffed the air. "You suppose those Mystic Knights are hiding from us . . . afraid?"

Ice Lord replied, "As well they should be. We'll crush them!"

Behind him, Lightning Bat's voice was nearly a shriek. "We must take them before they encounter that dragon again. We don't want to let it have all the fun destroying them!"

The other Evil Sentinels broke into harsh, cruel laughter. As they did, Aideen the fairy popped into view. The Sea Serpent's laughter choked in his throat. "Hey, that's that little fairy who's been helping the Mystic Knights."

"I'll take care of her!" the Rock Wolf snarled.

The Evil Sentinel lunged at Aideen, but the speedy

fairy kept flying out of reach. "Listen to me! Listen to me!" she called out.

"Listen?" the Ice Lord laughed. "We don't have time to listen. We're on our way to take care of your four friends."

"That's why I'm here," Aideen said. "They're not my friends anymore!"

The Lightning Bat became interested. "Oh?"

The fairy nodded. "They never appreciated what I did for them. They wouldn't even listen to my plan. So now I don't care what happens to them."

The Lightning Bat crouched down close to Aideen. His foul breath washed over her. "We appreciate you, little fairy. Why don't you join our side?"

Aideen stood as tall as she could manage. "I don't want to be on anyone's side. I just want to get even."

The Ice Lord shoved the Lightning Bat aside. "Enough talk! Tell us where they are right now or off with you!"

Aideen smiled gleefully. "Follow me."

The fairy zipped away at magical speed, and the Evil Sentinels trudged along behind her. She led them through the forest to a wide clearing covered with wildflowers. On the far side of the field the Evil Sentinels could see the Mystic Knights yelling at one another in loud voices. They seemed to be arguing about something, and obviously did not expect an attack.

"Now we have them," the Sea Serpent hissed.

"Good-bye, then," Aideen said. "I don't want to be here when things get ugly." With a magical pop, the fairy vanished.

The Sea Serpent squinted into the distance. "We could circle around the forest and sneak up on them."

The Ice Lord shook his skeletal head. "What for? They're without their armor and we have their weapons. I say we attack straight on."

The Lightning Bat drew his Bat-el-Axe. "This will be like spearing fish in a barrel."

Yelling in one loud, blood-chilling voice, the four Evil Sentinels charged across the field.

And froze in place.

Aideen had led them into the pixie field!

Turn to page 8

78

"Pyre may be important," Deirdre said, "but my father's kingdom is in danger right now. We already know that the four of us can handle the Temran army. I say we fight them off!"

The others agreed. Without waiting for the rest of Conchobar's soldiers, the Mystic Knights set out for the northern border, where Maeve's army was said to be gathering.

As they hurried northward, the Mystic Knights plunged into a thick mist. With each step the mist seemed to grow thicker and darker, until they could barely see their hands in front of their faces.

"This mist is as thick as an Ogre's skin," Angus grumbled.

"Pay it no mind," Ivar replied. "In my homeland, the mist gathers so thick that we bundle it like straw and sell it at the market. It can't hurt you."

"Unless it makes you lose your way," Deirdre said. She stopped short. "Does anyone know exactly where the northern border is?"

"This way," said Rohan, pointing to the left.

"This way," said Ivar, pointing to the right.

"We're lost." Angus kicked a rock in frustration. "This mist was sent by Maeve, I'll wager."

Deirdre shrugged. "Well, there's nothing to do but find our way out. Let's go."

They marched on through the mist for what seemed like hours. Finally, the thick gray clouds seemed to part and they found themselves standing on the shore of a sunny lake. The surface of the lake was as smooth and clear as glass.

"I didn't know there was a lake here," Rohan said.

"I didn't know I looked so tired," Angus said, staring at his reflection in the clear water. "I definitely need my beauty sleep."

"These reflections are so clear," Deirdre noticed. In the still water she could see herself perfectly. As the other heroes looked into the water, they could see themselves too.

Rohan studied his reflection. It was very lifelike. Almost too lifelike. He frowned.

But the reflection smiled.

"By the fire of dragons!" he cried, stumbling back.

His move saved his life. His reflection suddenly reached up, its hands breaking through the water, and tried to pull him in. The others stepped back, too, as their reflections clutched at them.

"The lake is enchanted!" Rohan cried.

"And it's coming after us!" Deirdre added.

The reflections rose up out of the water. Four figures that looked exactly like Rohan, Deirdre, Angus, and Ivar waded out of the lake, shaking off a few droplets. The four false heroes drew weapons that matched the four weapons of the Mystic Knights.

"It's a fight they want," Rohan said.

"And it's a fight they'll get!" Ivar declared. He leaped forward to attack his own enchanted double. But the false Ivar blocked the Barbed Trident with a Barbed Trident of his own. The two Ivars were soon locked in furious combat.

Rohan barely drew the Sword of Kells in time to defend himself from an assault by his own double. He dodged one blow, then another. He knew he had to end this battle quickly if the Mystic Knights were to find Maeve's army. Sliding away from another blow by the false Rohan, the true Rohan prepared his best move—one that never failed him. He faked a low strike with the Sword of Kells, then quickly changed direction and swung high in an attack that was impossible to defend.

But the false Rohan blocked it! The enchanted creature then kicked Rohan in the chest, and sent him staggering backward.

Deirdre unleashed her Whirlwind Crossbow at her double, only to find that the false Deirdre had done exactly the same thing. Beside her, Angus pounded his twin with a flurry of blows from the Terra Mace, but the false Angus seemed to read his mind, blocking every blow.

"This is impossible!" Angus shouted. "It's like they know what we're going to do before we do it!"

"That's it!" Rohan said, narrowly avoiding a strike that would have removed his head from his shoulders. "We're fighting ourselves!"

"I can see that!" Angus snapped back. "Although I think I'm better looking."

"Rohan's right!" Deirdre said. "We can't defeat them because they're us! They know exactly what we're going to do!"

"This is the first time," Ivar said, panting with exhaustion, "that I wished I wasn't so good a fighter!"

"What do we do?" Angus asked.

For a moment Rohan wasn't sure, but then he realized that the answer was obvious. "Trade opponents!" he yelled. Quick as lightning, he abandoned his own twin and rushed at Angus's. The false Angus was startled, but tried to crush him with his Terra Mace. However, Rohan did not use the same brute force that Angus had used. He dodged the blow and slipped inside the false creature's guard, striking out with the Sword of Kells. The blade found its mark, and in an instant the false Angus vanished in a cloud of mist.

"Well done!" Ivar cheered. He turned from his own image to attack the false Deirdre. The enchanted creation aimed its own Whirlwind Crossbow at him, but Ivar fired the Barbed Trident. The lightning bolt sizzled right through the center of the whirlwind and struck the false Deirdre, turning her into water vapor.

The real Deirdre had already aimed her own Whirlwind Crossbow at the false Rohan. The magical creation tried to fry her with the flaming Sword of Kells, but Deirdre's whirlwind drove the flames back at him. Swallowed up by fire, the false twin transformed into steam.

Angus, meanwhile, had already taken care of the false Ivar with a shattering blow of the Terra Mace. The mace struck the enchanted creature like a hand slapping water. There was a splash, and the false image scattered into tiny droplets.

Angus heaved a sigh of relief. "Well, that's something you don't see every day."

"At least it's over," Ivar panted. "Now, to find Maeve's army—"

"No," Rohan said.

Deirdre raised an eyebrow. "What do you mean, Rohan?"

The young hero was staring across the lake. "I don't know if Maeve created this enchantment or not, but I think it's some kind of warning. By choosing to fight Maeve's army, we're only fighting ourselves."

Deirdre considered this. "You mean we're making things more difficult?"

"Exactly," Rohan said. "We have to keep our minds on our real goal."

Turn to page 5